BY D: ce JONeS

Jig and Saw arrived home from school,
and placed their bags on a nearby stool.
Their timing was perfect just in time for tea,
so they sat down to eat at half past three.

Fruit pie eaten that Mum had baked,
then outside to play on their brand new skates.
Fun-time scuppered when it started to rain,
so back indoors to find another game.

Jig opened the door on a cupboard so worn,
and discovered a box with a lid that was torn.
The cover was damaged and Saw sensed some trouble,
as her brother revealed a word game called "Strubble".

A board full of squares was laid on the floor,
word tiles poured out... the Y was worth four.
Game pieces checked and Jig scratched his head,
"Two tiles are missing... the X and the Z!"

Jig and Saw looked inside the green bag,
to check if the pieces were stuck in the rag.
They peered in further then toppled inside,
and started their journey... oh what a ride!

A long tunnel spiralled and they continued to fall,
it was quite frightening... not funny at all.
A distant light shone and both held out a hand,
as the swirling stopped... they'd found Strubble Land.

A King and Queen with faces quite red,
welcomed Jig and Saw... "We've lost X and Z!"
The puzzles enquired "Where could they be?"
then a tile valued one pointed up at a tree.

X and Z spied down from the branches,
grumbled and groaned as the crowd cast their glances.
Jig and Saw shouted "Look... there they are!"
as the Strubbles below yelled a thankful "Hurrah!"

Jig and Saw realised the letters felt neglected,
played no part in Strubble so were always dejected.
They climbed up a ladder to the word tiles so shy,
and persuaded them down to join letter Y.

A new game of Strubble was soon under way,
with X and Z invited to play.
Jig and Saw utilised them to their best,
they made up great words like Xylophone and Zest.

The game ended well with everyone pleased,
because X and Z were no longer teased.
"Time to leave!" Jig and Saw rubbed their eyes,
as the Strubbles gathered to say their goodbyes.

The green bag reopened and they jumped inside,
for their homeward journey down a long slide.
The swirling grew stronger and they reached the end,
of an amazing adventure that helped two new friends.

Back home safely... they met sister Flo,
who questioned their absence "Where did you go?"
With a shrug of the shoulders they made an excuse,
"We've been down the shops to buy apple juice!"

Flo gave a look of disbelief,
then left to find Mum and report their mischief.
The coast was now clear for Jig and Saw,
to put Strubble in the cupboard and close the door.

Saw pulled Jig's arm and pointed down,
at two smiling word tiles without a frown.
On the floor facing up were the missing Z and X,
Jig and Saw wondered "What adventure is next?"